Cassidy

A Chill in the Air

in the

Nature Poems for Fall and Winter

Poems by
John Frank

Illustrated by
Mike Reed

Simon & Schuster Books for Young Readers
New York London Toronto Sydney Singapore

Signs

Songbirds hushing,
Maples blushing,
Rivers rushing—
Fall is here.

Fall

Fall sets fire
To the tips of trees,
And fans the flames
With an icy breeze.

Mushrooms

Along the shady forest floor
As summer's long days wane,
The mushrooms pop up, wearing hats
To shed the autumn rain.

Blackberry Picking

In early fall the blackberry vines
were full of berries to take.
I picked enough to fatten
all the pies we planned to bake.
Yet not a drop of filling
did those juicy berries make:
I carried home two empty pails
and one full tummy ache.

Words

In the dawn
that chills my bones
and numbs my face
from ear to ear,
I see each word I speak
take flight,
a whiff of fog,
then disappear.

A Cold October Night

If any witches plan to ride
their broomsticks through this cold night air,
they'd best make sure beneath their gowns
they're wearing thermal underwear.

Late Fall

Many leaves
turn
few

to let the
low sun
through.

A Sprinkling of Snow

It hardly snowed at all last night
although I hoped it would.
I wished for lots and lots of snow,
but wishing did no good.
With so much snow my snowman
would have grown and grown and grown.
But now he's scarcely bigger than
a three-scoop ice-cream cone.

Fall's End

I watched the leaves come boating down
On streams of autumn air,
And when the last gold leaf shook free
And left the branches bare,
I ran to catch it in my hands
Before it touched the ground,
And brought it home to keep among
The treasures I have found.

Brrrrr
   dead leaves
   frost heaves
   icy eaves

   long sleeves

Winter

When winter waves
its magic wand
we all lace on
our shiny skates,
and glide upon
the frozen pond
in circles, lines,
and figure eights.

Footprints

As I am walking
in the snow
my footprints follow
where I go,
and make a long
and winding track
that leads me home
when I turn back.

Thief

The winter wind's a clever thief:
He'll join with you in play,
Then slip his hand inside your coat
And steal the warmth away.

Polar Vacation

It's ten degrees below outside
and positively foul,
just perfect for a polar bear
with sunscreen and a towel.

Freezing Rain

A soft rain falls
Through the winter air
That chills the mountain pass,
And clings to the trees
That crown the hills
And turns them into glass.

Icicles

Crystal
pendants
slowly
grow
from
tiny
drops
of
melted
snow.

Moods

Sometimes
winter whispers
with stillness
and frail light.

Sometimes
winter roars
with storms
of terrifying might.

Winter Sun

It's dark
in the morning
when I get up,
and at night
when I rest my head,
for the sun
rises late
each winter day,
and soon goes
back to bed.

Winter Moon

This wintry night
the full moon's glow
spills gold on mountains
draped with snow,
and coaxes shadows
from the trees
whose bare limbs brave
the winter's freeze.

Scarcity

The earth grows stingy
in the winter wild
when the wind blows cold
and the snow lies deep—

her creatures scour
for bits of food,
or still their hunger
with weeks of sleep.

Winter's End

buds on branches slowly swelling

a stirring in a winter dwelling

days are longer

the sun feels stronger

the cold is fading

spring is near

For Yan Qiu
—J. F.

To Jane, Alex, and Joe
—M. R.

SIMON & SCHUSTER BOOKS FOR YOUNG READERS
An imprint of Simon & Schuster Children's Publishing Division
1230 Avenue of the Americas, New York, New York 10020
Text copyright © 2003 by John Frank
Illustrations copyright © 2003 by Mike Reed
SIMON & SCHUSTER BOOKS FOR YOUNG READERS is a trademark of Simon & Schuster.
Book design by Greg Stadnyk
The text for this book is set in Highlander and Gill Sans.
The illustrations are rendered in acrylic.
Manufactured in the United States of America
2 4 6 8 10 9 7 5 3 1
Library of Congress Cataloging-in-Publication Data
Frank, John.
A chill in the air : nature poems for fall and winter / John Frank ; illustrated by Mike Reed.—1st ed.
p. cm.
Summary: A collection of short poems which reflect the seasonal changes as fall arrives and slowly turns to winter,
winter brings storms and shorter days, then finally begins to fade into a hint of spring.
ISBN 0-689-83923-5
1. Nature—Juvenile poetry. 2. Autumn—Juvenile poetry. 3. Winter—Juvenile poetry. 4. Children's poetry, American.
[1. Nature—Poetry. 2. Autumn—Poetry. 3. Winter—Poetry. 4. American poetry.] I. Reed, Mike, 1951– ill. II. Title.
PS3556.R33425 C48 2003
811.'54—dc21   2002036491

The poems *Fall, Freezing Rain, Winter Moon,* and *Icicles* were previously published by The Cricket Magazine Group.